For the twelve dancing princesses:
Liza Dolmetsch, Nicky Dyal, Sukari Jones, Laura Kasson,
Liz Kushner, Lizbeth Latham, Alyson Piastra, Stacey Polishook,
Tessa Rexroat, Jannett Santana, Maria Stillo,
and Amanda White
—N.W.

For my husband, Tom, who is forever sweeping
me off my feet
—M.G.

Little, Brown and Company

Time Warner Book Group
1271 Avenue of the Americas, New York, NY 10020
Visit our Web site at www.lb-kids.com

First Edition

Library of Congress Cataloging-in-Publication Data

Willard, Nancy.
Sweep dreams / by Nancy Willard ; illustrated by Mary GrandPré. — 1st ed.
p. cm.
Summary: A man who loves a magical, dancing broom learns how to make her happy, finds her
after she is stolen, and finally sets her free and hopes that someday she will return home.
ISBN 0-316-94008-9
[1. Brooms and brushes—Fiction. 2. Magic—Fiction.] I. GrandPré, Mary, ill. II. Title.

PZ7.W6553Sw2004
[E]—dc21   2002041635

10 9 8 7 6 5 4 3 2 1

SC
Manufactured in China

The illustrations for this book were done in oil washes and colored pencil on board.
The text was set in Gararond Medium, and the display type
was hand-lettered by Mary GrandPré.

Book design by Alyssa Morris

Sweep Dreams

by Nancy Willard ✦ Illustrated by Mary GrandPré

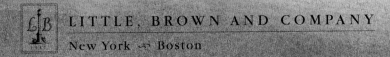

LITTLE, BROWN AND COMPANY

New York ✦ Boston

*T*here was once a man who fell in love with a broom.

The broom stood all alone at the end of an aisle, between the mayonnaise and the frozen foods. Her broomstraws were as red as if she'd swept up a sunset, and her handle still showed traces of bark.

The man did not need a broom, but he could not bear to leave this one in the store.

When he carried it to the checkout counter, the woman who worked at the register could not find a price on it.

"It looks handmade," she said. "We don't sell handmade brooms with red bristles."
"Where did it come from?" asked the man.
"Who knows? Take it with you and give it a good home."
"Thank you," said the man.

And he took the broom home.

But when he brought her into the living room, the broom looked much too beautiful for sweeping. So he set her in a corner where he could admire her.

Days passed. The broom looked more and more unhappy. Her bristles drooped. Her handle shed what was left of her bark. The man did not know whether to call a doctor or a veterinarian.

First he called the doctor. The line was busy, so he hung up and called the veterinarian, who told him he should come over right away.

The veterinarian examined the broom from top to bottom.

"Its bristles feel too soft. Does it get enough exercise?"

"Oh, I could never sweep with a broom this beautiful," said the man.

"Why, there's your problem," said the veterinarian. "Who ever heard of a broom not sweeping? Sweeping is what they love."

So every morning the man swept his front steps, and every evening he swept his kitchen floor, and once a week he swept the bedroom and the hall and the living room that let in the light and gave him a grand view of the hill.

And every night he put the broom back in her corner.

One night he woke up and heard *shhhhh swshhhhh ssssswhhhhhh.* It sounded like a frog in bedroom slippers, or a peacock hauling its tail in a paper bag, or the fog putting on an overcoat. *Shhhhh swshhhhh ssssswhhhhhh.*

The man peeked into the living room. By the light of the full moon, the broom was sweeping.

"My broom is a sweepwalker," said the man to himself. "I'll have to keep an eye on her."

He picked her up, but she kept right on sweeping. How
graceful she was! Together they swept up and down the room,
into the kitchen, and down the hall, and the floors they swept
gleamed in the moonlight.

One neighbor saw them and told another neighbor, who told another neighbor, "Isn't that wonderful? There's a dancing broom in the neighborhood." The broom didn't mind. Children watched her from their windows before they fell asleep. Grown-ups sat out on their porches and watched the broom sweep the man's front walk. Afterward she rested against an old hickory tree at the edge of the yard until he came to fetch her.

One morning, a stranger stopped to watch. Day after day he came to watch, until the neighbors paid no attention to him. Day after day the stranger moved closer and closer. Day after day the broom swept up and down the walk alone, and every evening she danced with the man who had found her . . .

Until the day she disappeared.

The man put a "missing broom" notice in the paper, and he hung signs on all the telephone poles:

Below the words he drew a picture of the broom sweeping his front walk.

But nobody called and nobody called and nobody called. At last the man went to a fortune-teller who specialized in finding lost things. She looked into her shining ball and shook her head.

"The stranger who stole your broom took her to a theater far from here and locked her in his kitchen. One night he heard *shhhhh swshhhhh sssswhhhhhh* and saw the broom sweeping all by herself.

"The next day he put up posters":

DON'T MISS
MARVELOUS
MARTHA
the only dancing
broom in
captivity!

"Crowds fought for the best seats. A hush fell over the
audience, and the spotlight came up on the broom.
But the broom did not dance.
The stranger gave her a little shake.
But the broom did not dance.
The crowd shouted, 'It's a fake!'"

"The stranger returned their money and threw your broom into the river."

"Oh, my poor broom!" exclaimed the man.

"You've come just in time," said the fortune-teller. "At the foot of the hill flows a river. Stand on its banks and look upstream, and when you see your broom, wade out and bring her ashore."

For two days the man stood on the banks of the river, and on the third day he spied red bristles bobbing up and down on the current.

He rushed out and grabbed her handle and brought her home and dried her out and stood her in her old corner.

"I will never let anyone steal you again," he said. "I will never let you out of my sight."

Night after night he listened for the *shhhhh swshhhhhh* of her bristles sweeping the floor. But the broom did not dance.

"Perhaps my broom is restless," said the man to himself. "She's seen the wide world."

The next day was rainy, and clouds hung over the hill. The man opened his front door, and the broom danced down the walk and up the hill and swept away the clouds.

Behind the clouds hung other clouds, and she swept those away also. And behind those clouds hung a raggedy rainbow. The broom swept up one side of the rainbow and down the other and polished it. When the rainbow disappeared, so did the broom.

That night the man watched the first evening star rise over the hill. He ate his supper and stood in his front yard and looked up at the Milky Way that spilled in a shining river over his head and at the Big Dipper, hanging in the great kitchen of the sky.

The broom swept back and forth between them. By dawn she
had swept all the stars from the floor of the night except one.

That star fell at the feet of the man who found her.
He keeps it in his kitchen window to light her way when
she wants to come home.